Follow the dotted lines with your finger and then use your pencil to trace them.

Follow the dotted lines with your finger and then use your pencil to trace them.

Follow the dotted lines with your finger and then use your pencil to trace them.

Trace the shapes to complete the pictures.
Then, decorate the pictures.

Trace the shapes to complete the pictures.
Then, decorate the pictures.

Trace the shapes to complete the pictures.
Then, decorate the pictures.

Trace the path to help the pirate get to his ship.

Trace the path to help the car drive home.

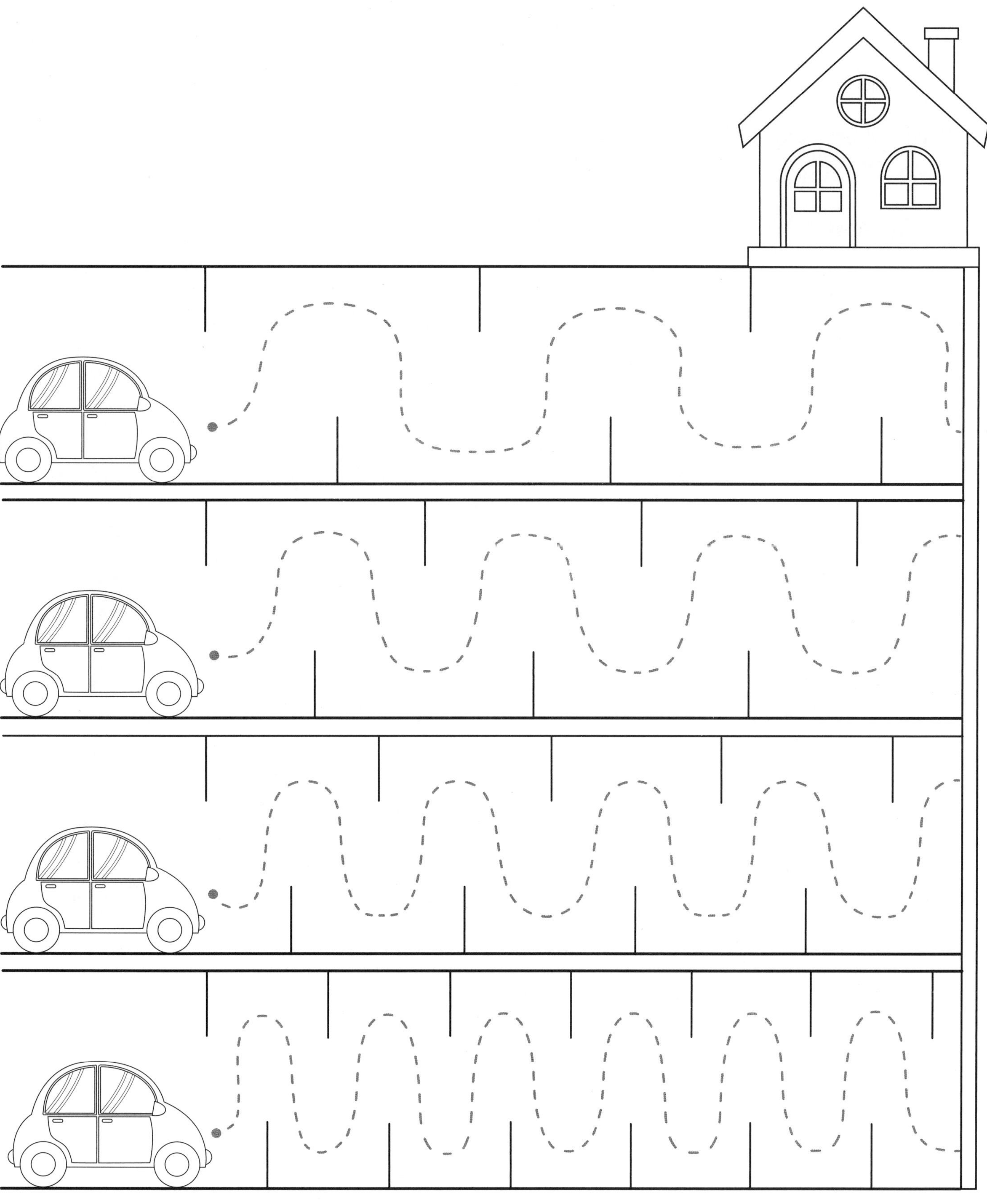

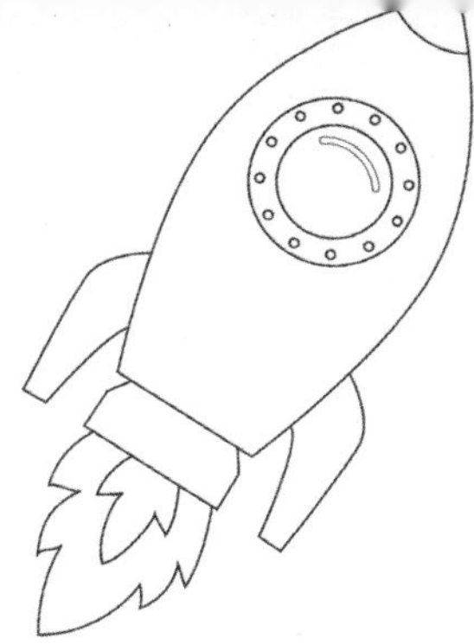

Trace the lines to follow the rocket around the stars.

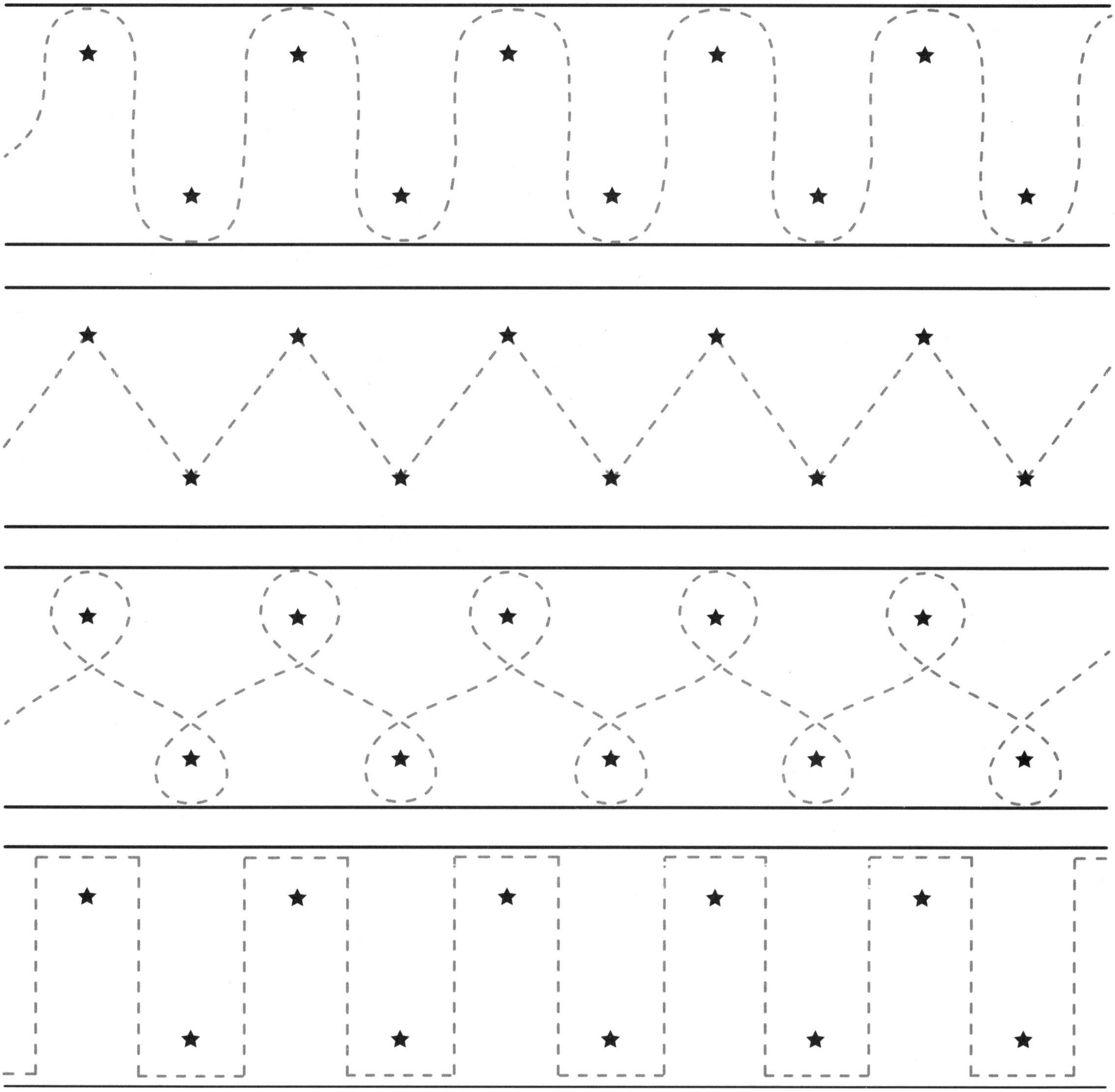

Trace around the outside of your hand.
Then, decorate the picture.

Trace the circle shapes and decorate them.
Then, trace the circles between the lines.

These letters are like circles.
Trace the letters.

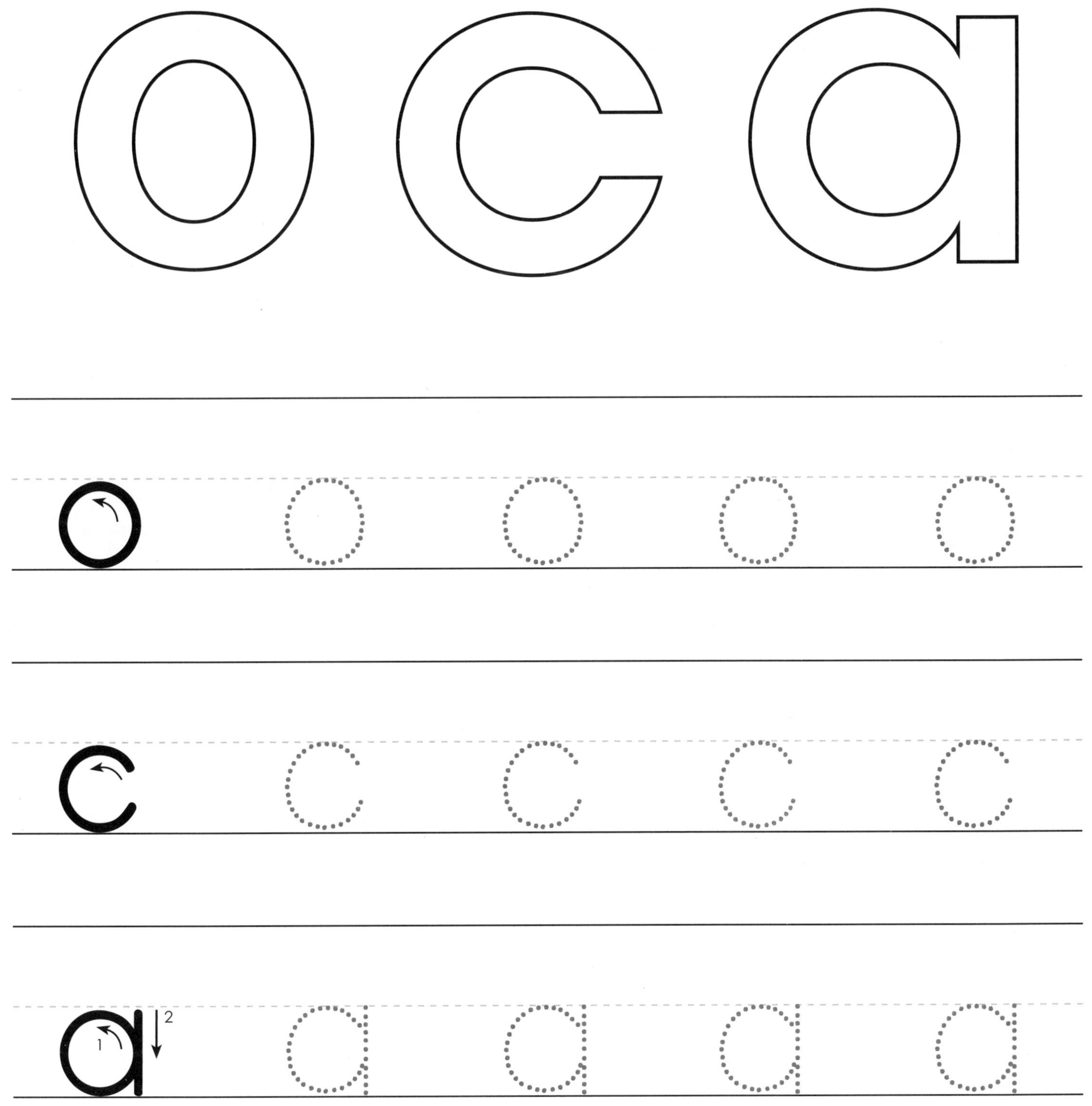

Trace the pictures with wavy lines and decorate the pictures. Then, trace the wavy shapes between the lines.

These letters are wavy and curly.
Trace the letters.

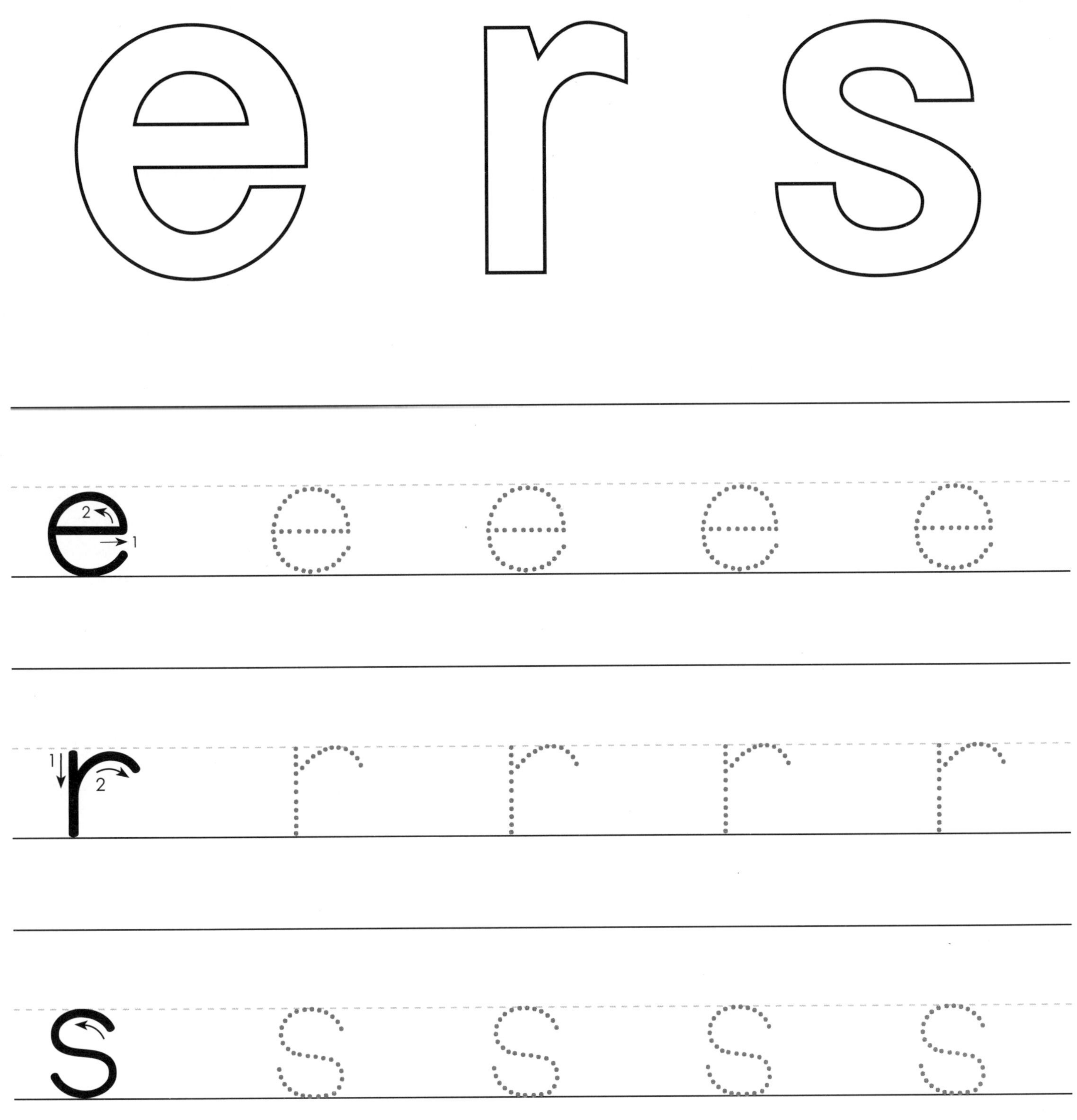

Trace the sticks, then decorate the pictures.
Then, trace the sticks between the lines.

These letters have stick shapes.
Trace the letters.

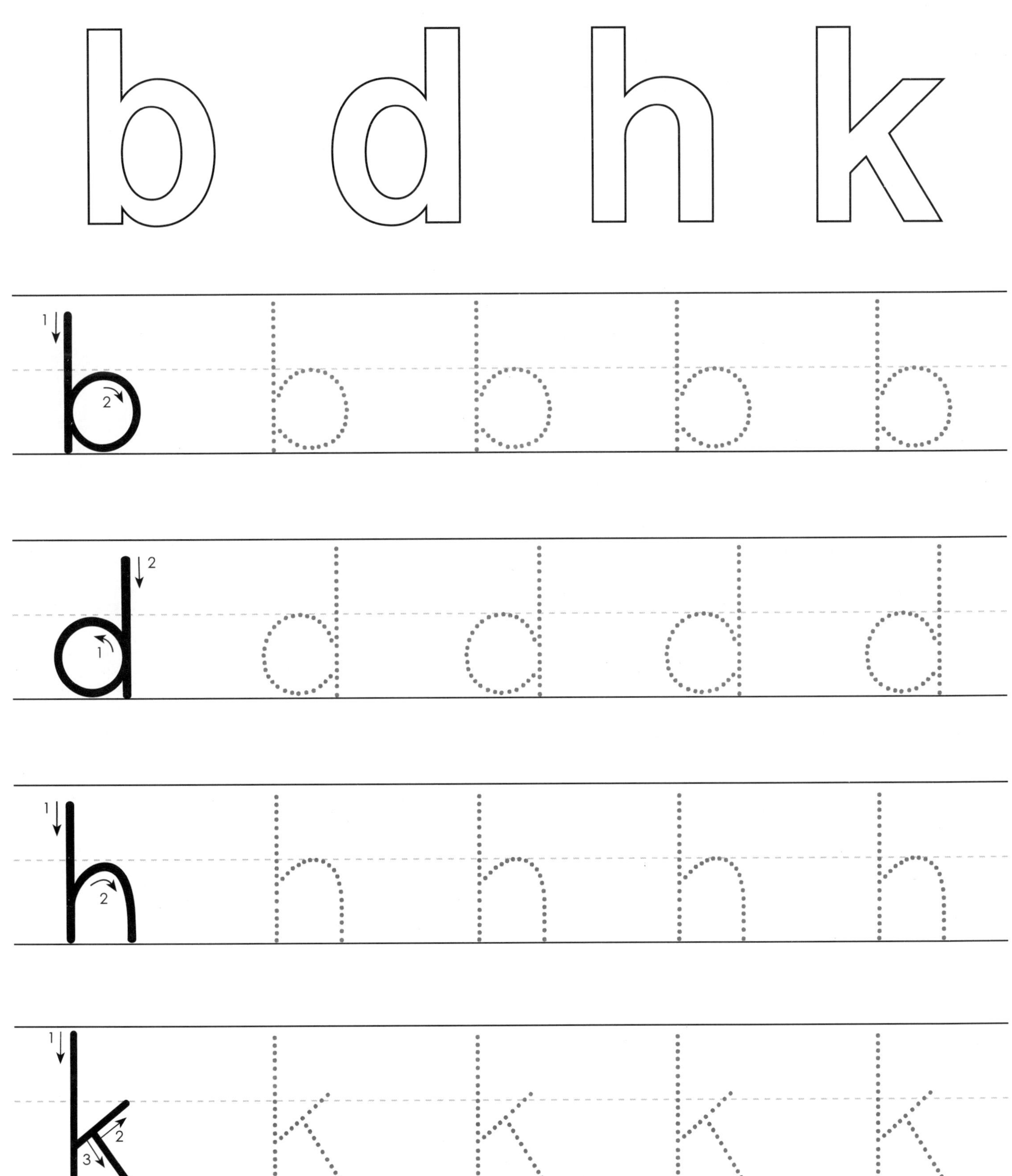

These letters have stick shapes too.
Trace the letters.

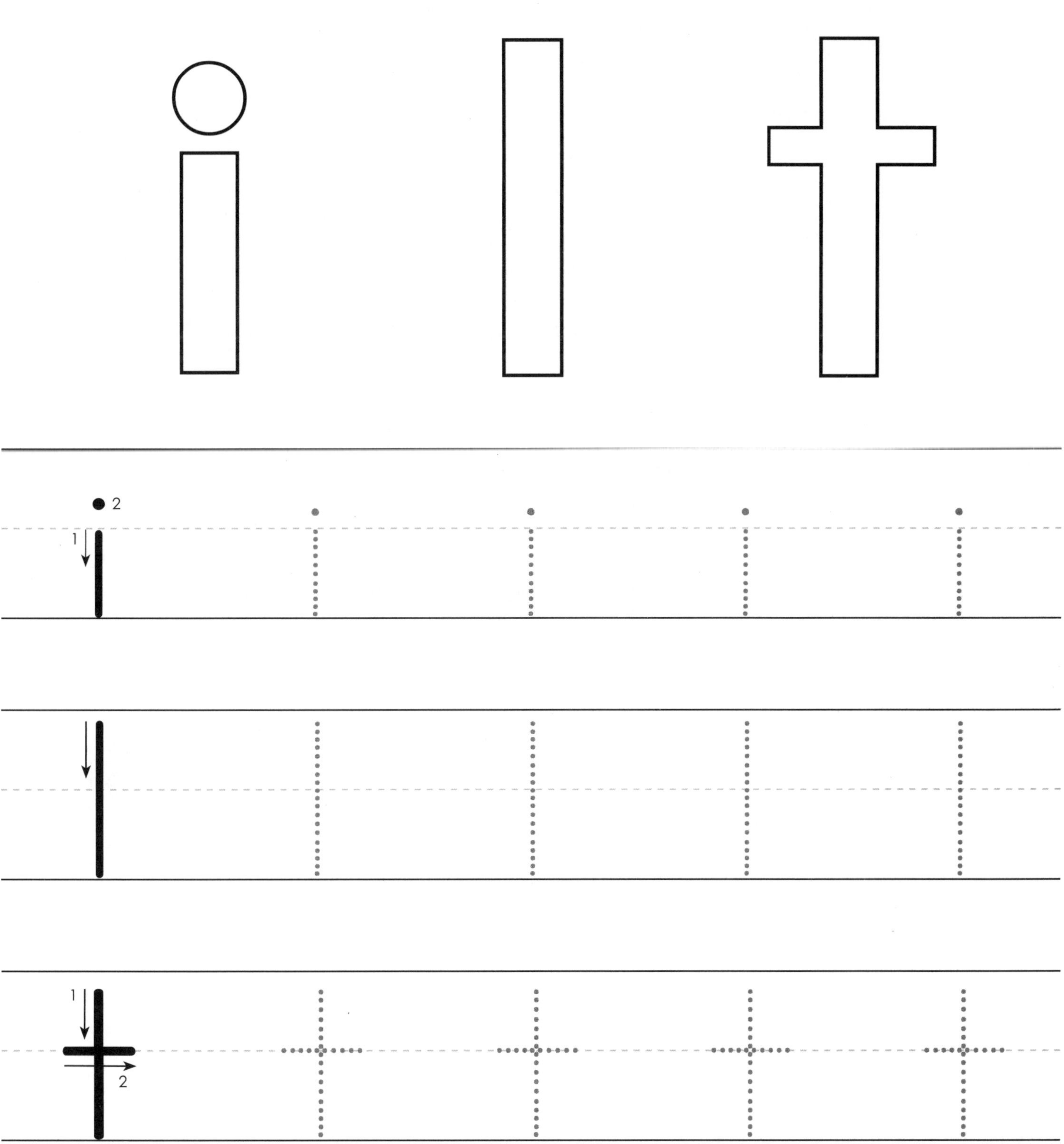

Here are some more letters with stick shapes.
Trace the letters.

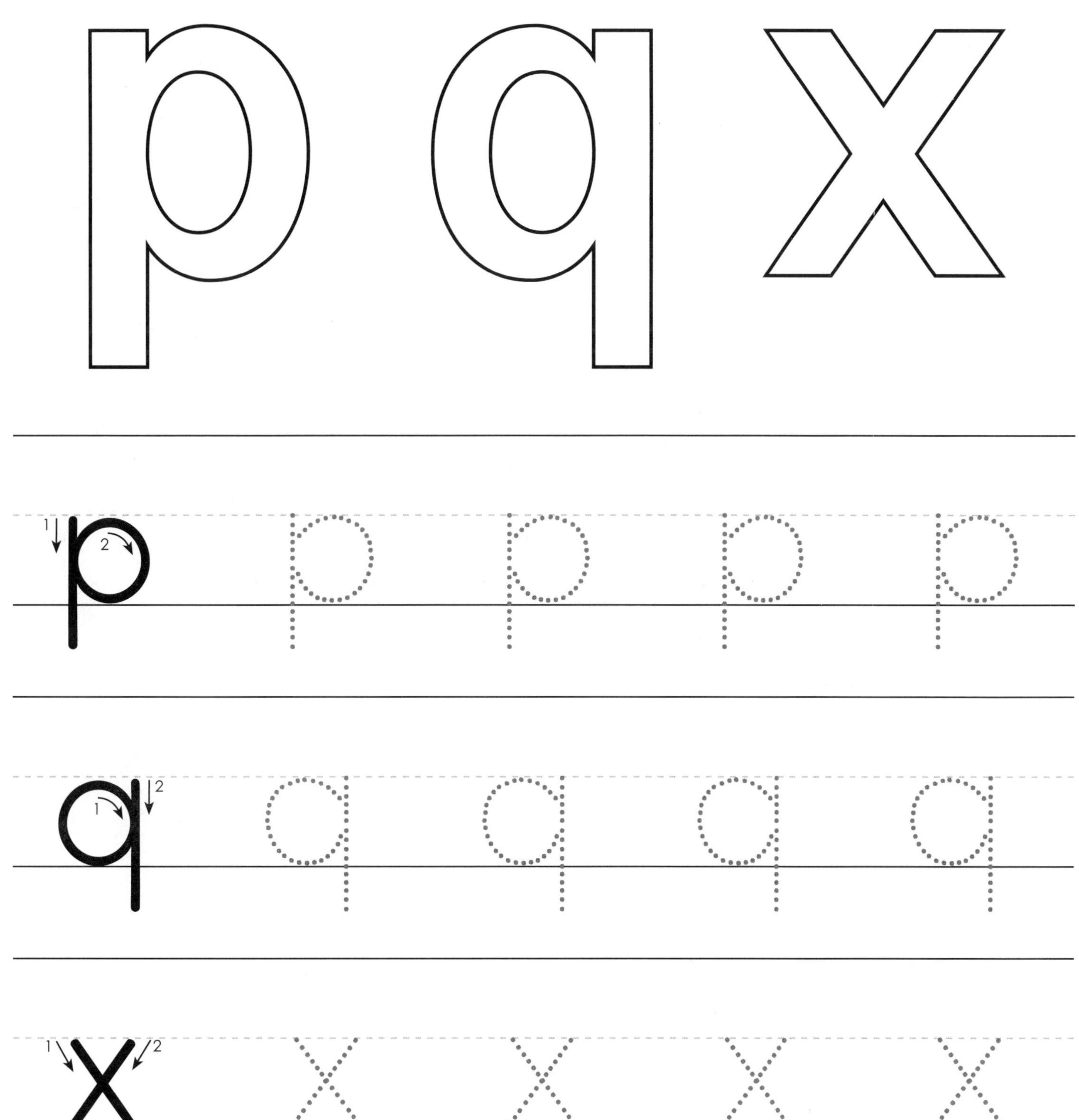

Trace the curly tails, then decorate the pictures. Then, trace the curly tails between the lines.

These letters have curly tails.
Trace the letters.

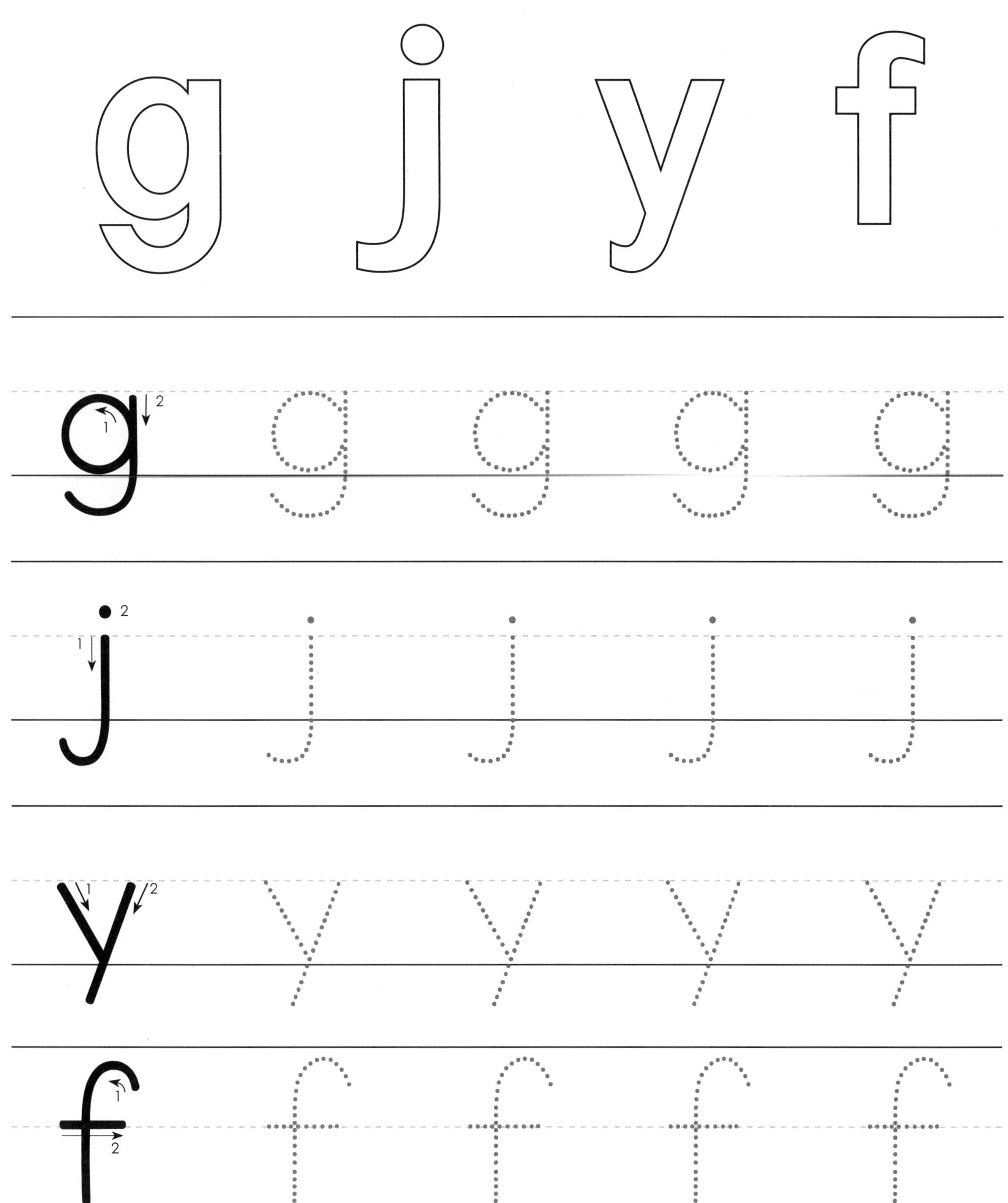

Trace the hill shapes, then decorate the pictures. Then, trace the hill shapes between the lines.

These letters have hill shapes.
Trace the letters.

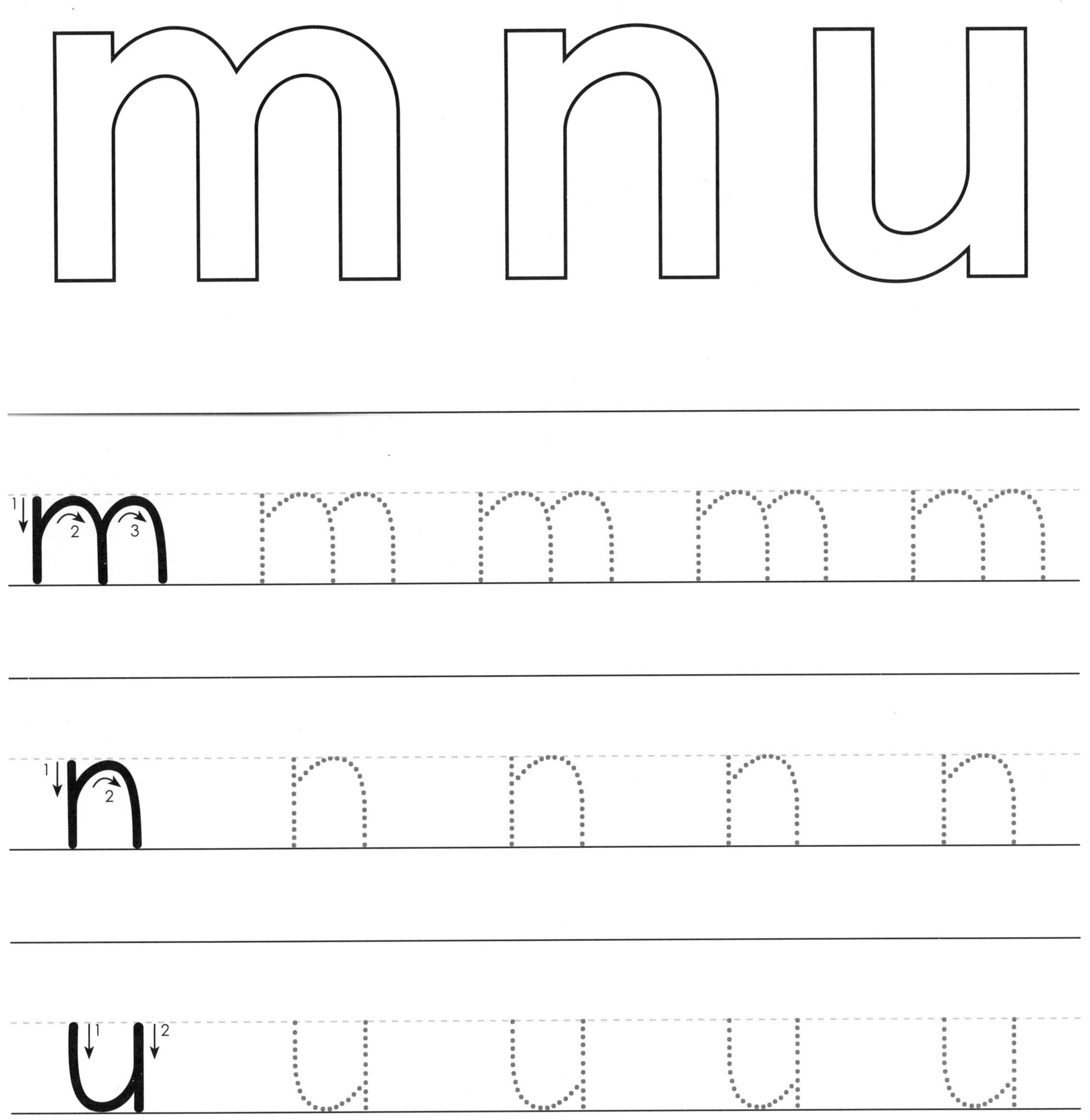

Trace the zig-zag shapes, then decorate the picture. Then, trace the zig zags between the lines.

These letters have zig-zag shapes.
Trace the letters.

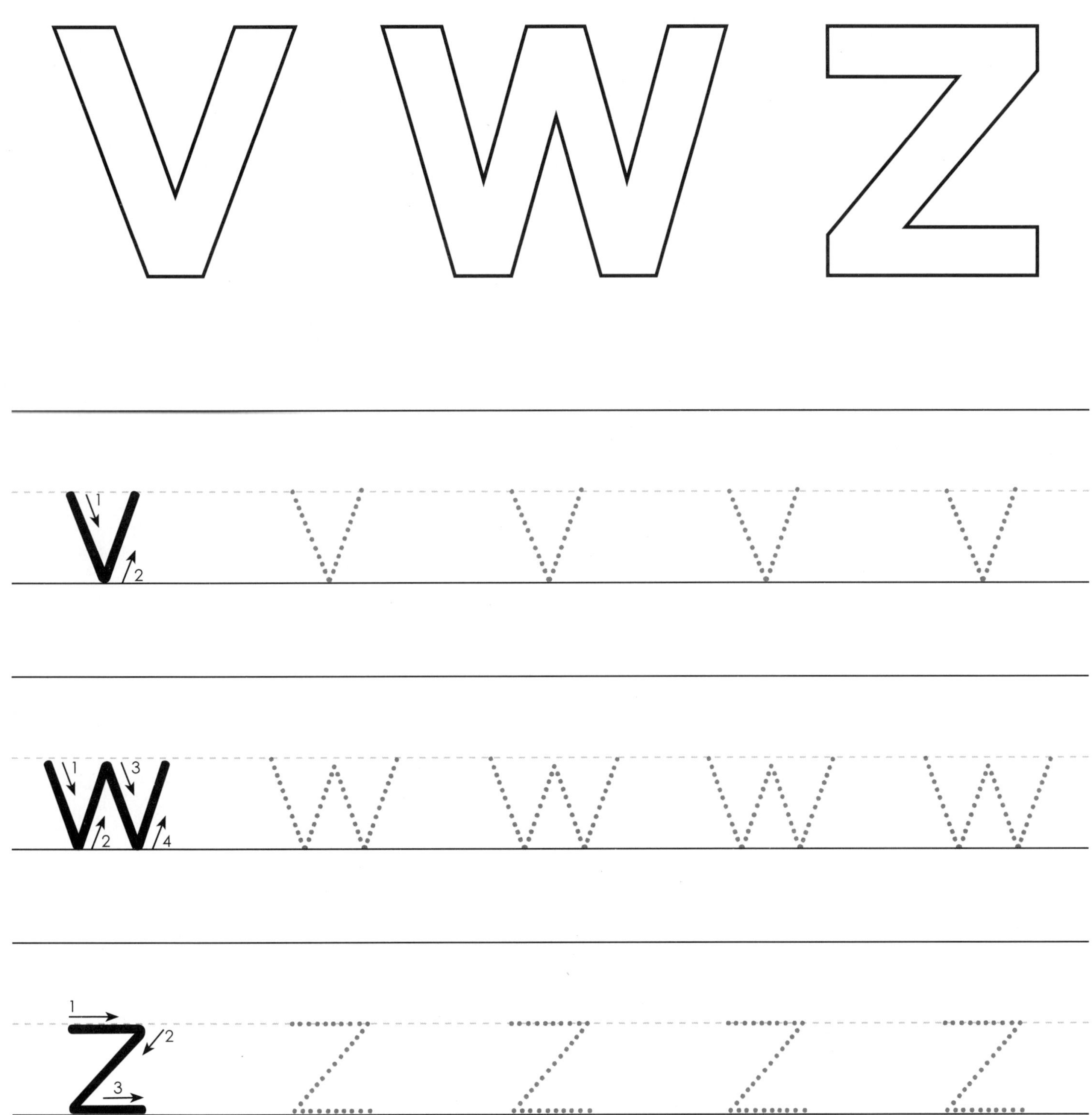

Write the alphabet.

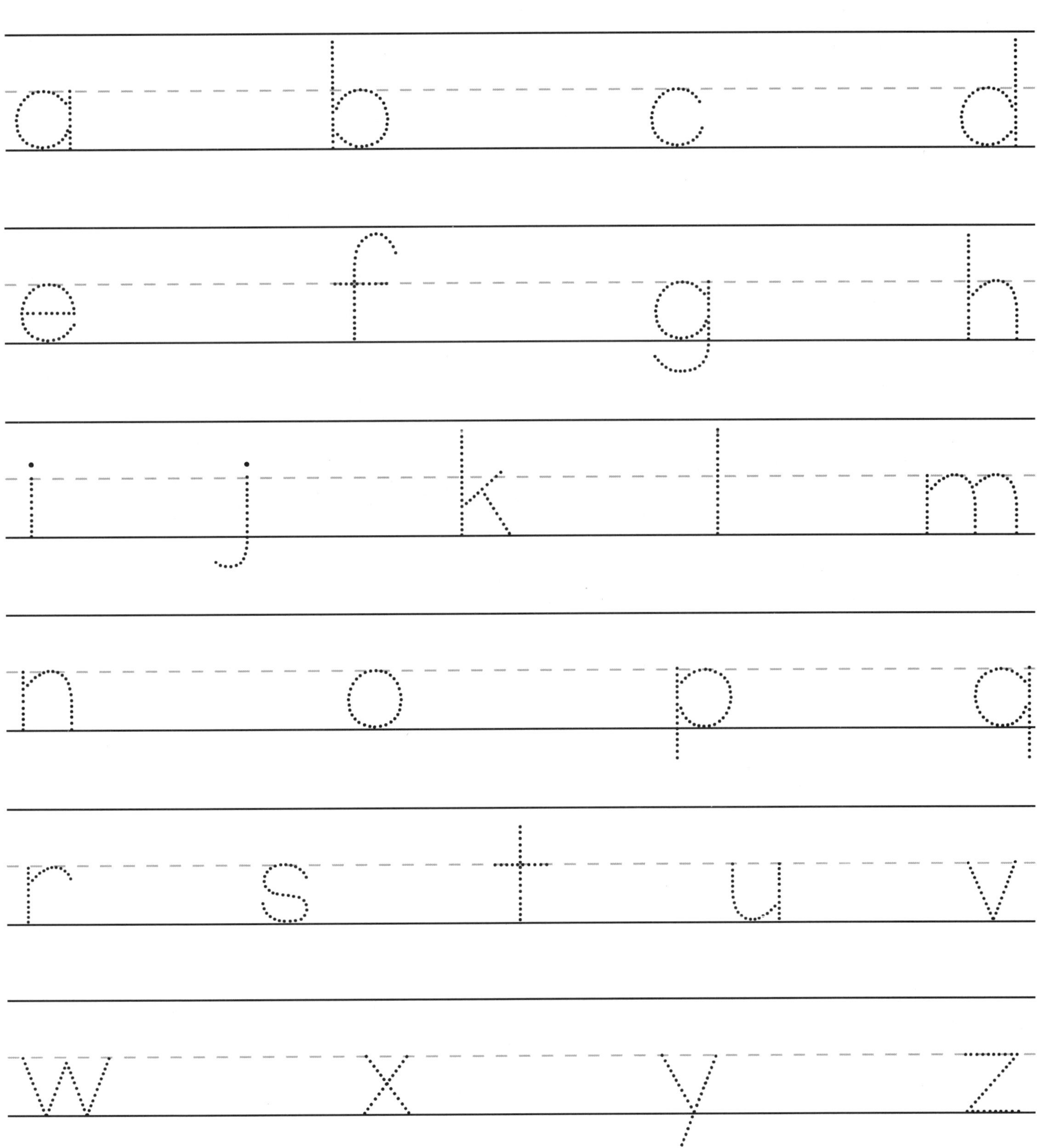

Write the letters **a** and **b**. Then write some words starting with those letters.

Write the letters **c** and **d**. Then write some words starting with those letters.

Write the letters **e** and **f**. Then write some words starting with those letters.

Write the letters **g** and **h**. Then write some words starting with those letters.

Write the letters **i** and **j**. Then write some words starting with those letters.

Write the letters **k** and **l**. Then write some words starting with those letters.

Write the letters **m** and **n**. Then write some words starting with those letters.

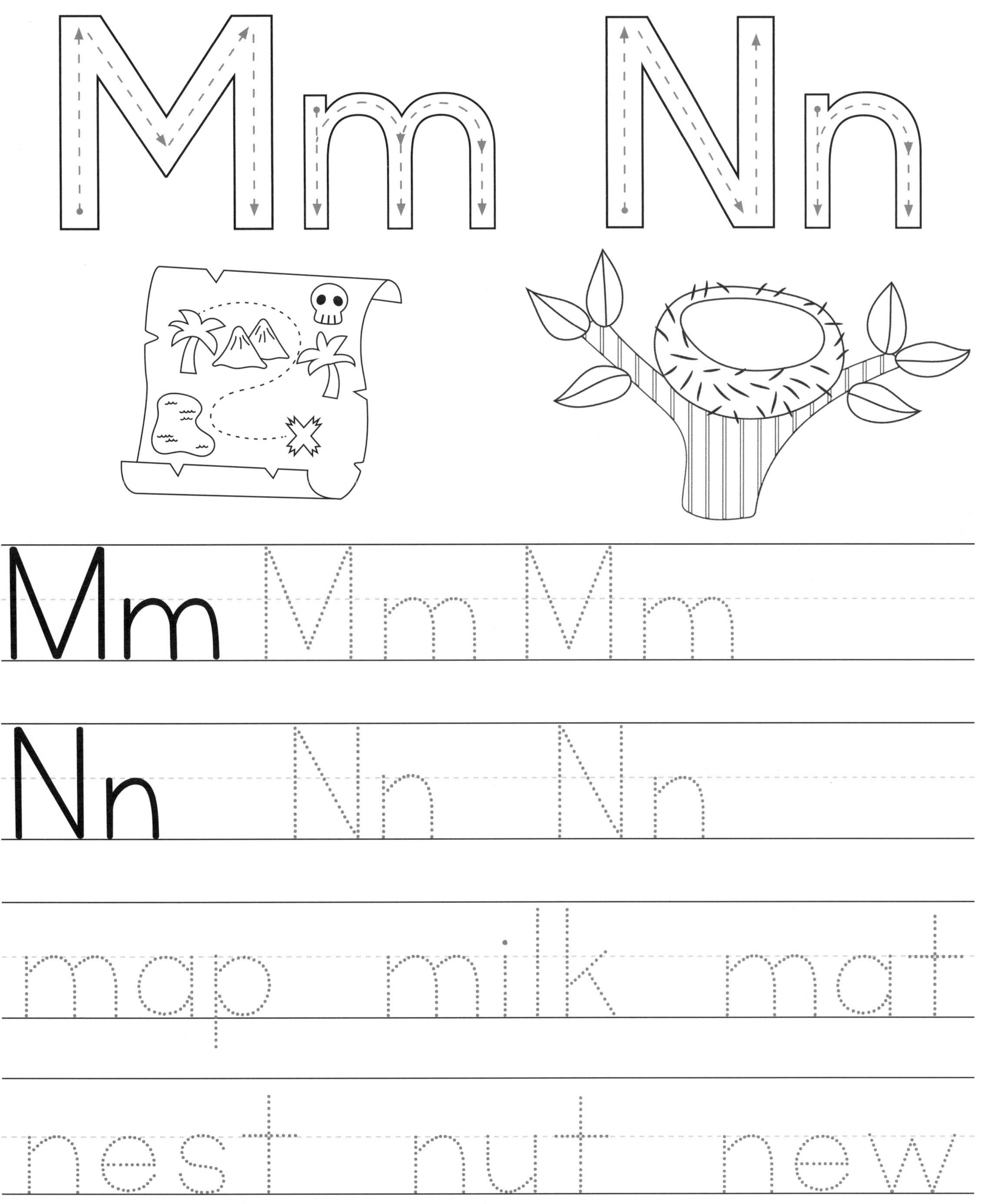

Write the letters **o** and **p**. Then write some words starting with those letters.

Write the letters **q** and **r**. Then write some words starting with those letters.

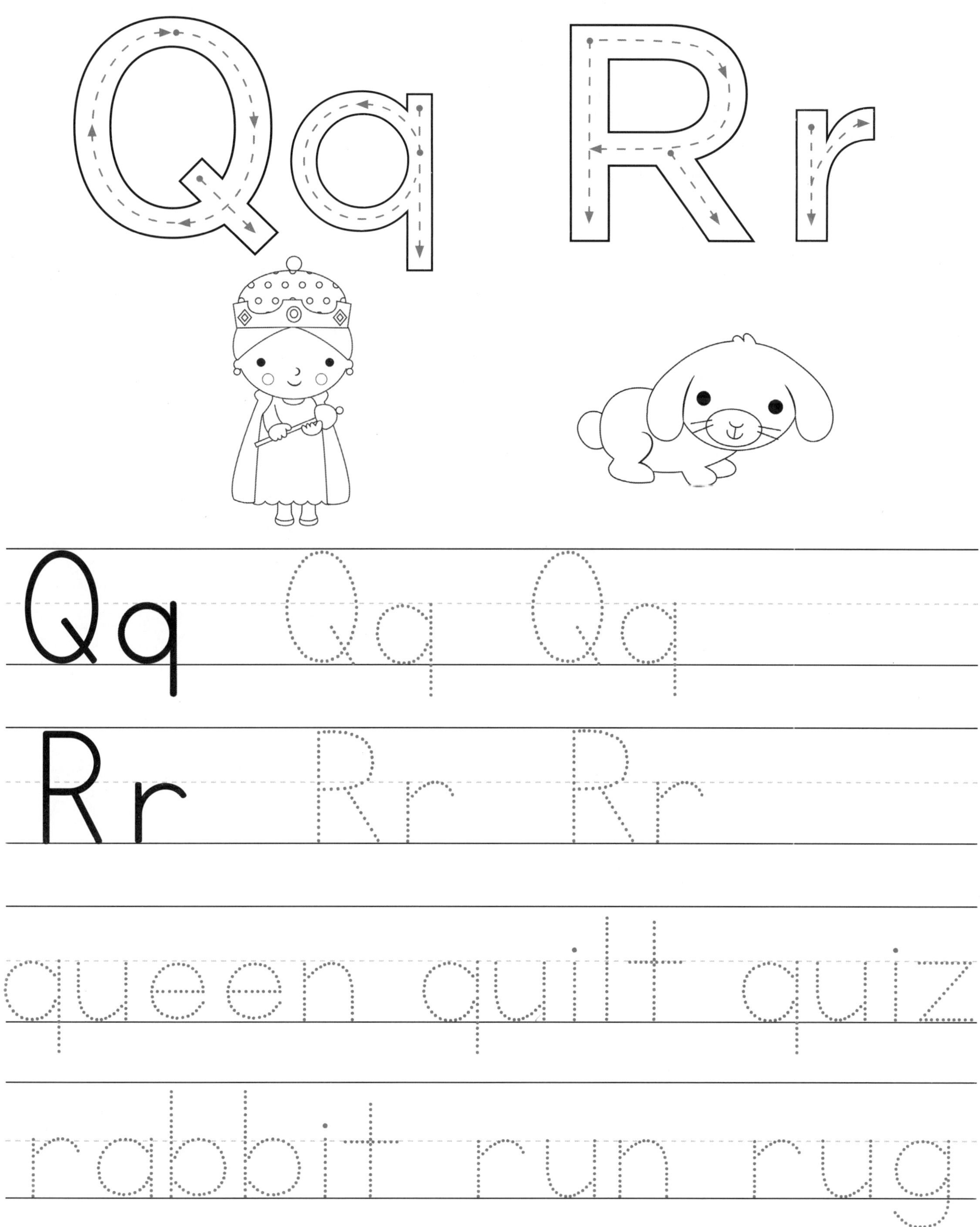

Write the letters **s** and **t**. Then write some words starting with those letters.

Write the letters **u** and **v**. Then write some words starting with those letters.

Write the letters **w** and **x**. Then write some words starting with those letters.

Write the letters **y** and **z**. Then write some words starting with those letters.

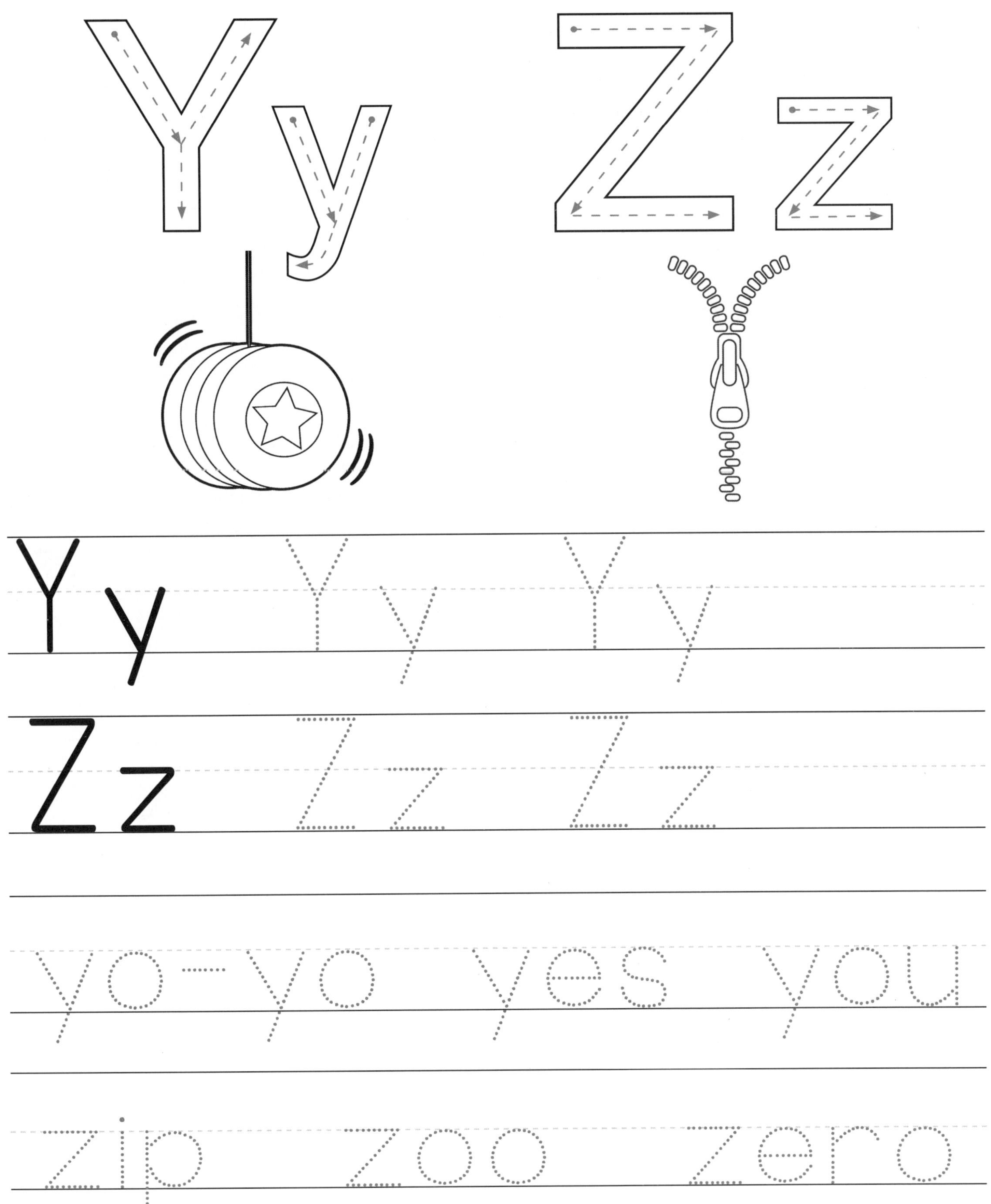

Trace the letters, then circle the one that is different.

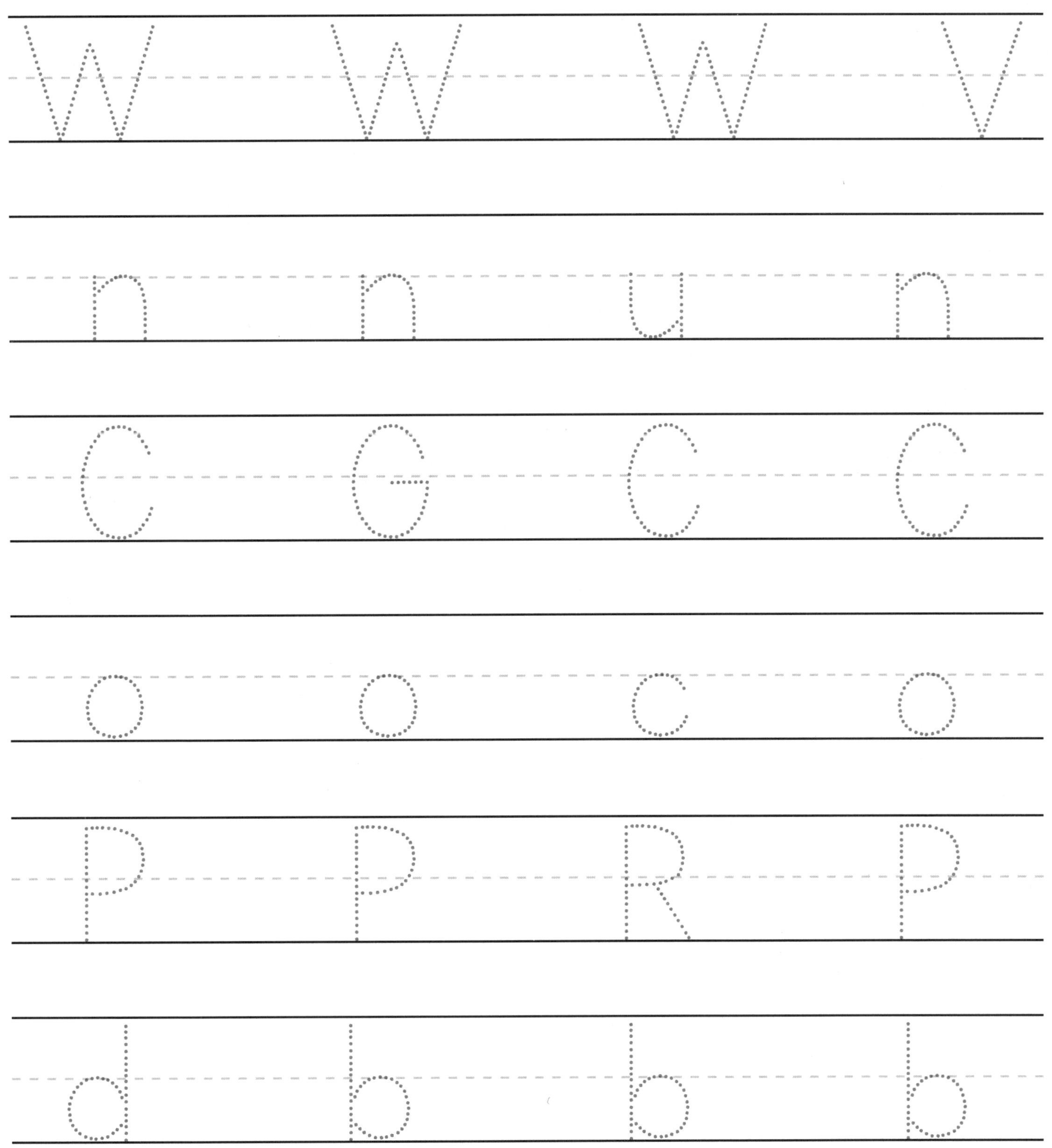

Write each word, then say the first letter of each word.

Write each word, then say the first letter of each word.

Trace the numbers, then decorate the pictures.

Trace the numbers, then decorate the pictures.

Trace the numbers, then decorate the pictures.

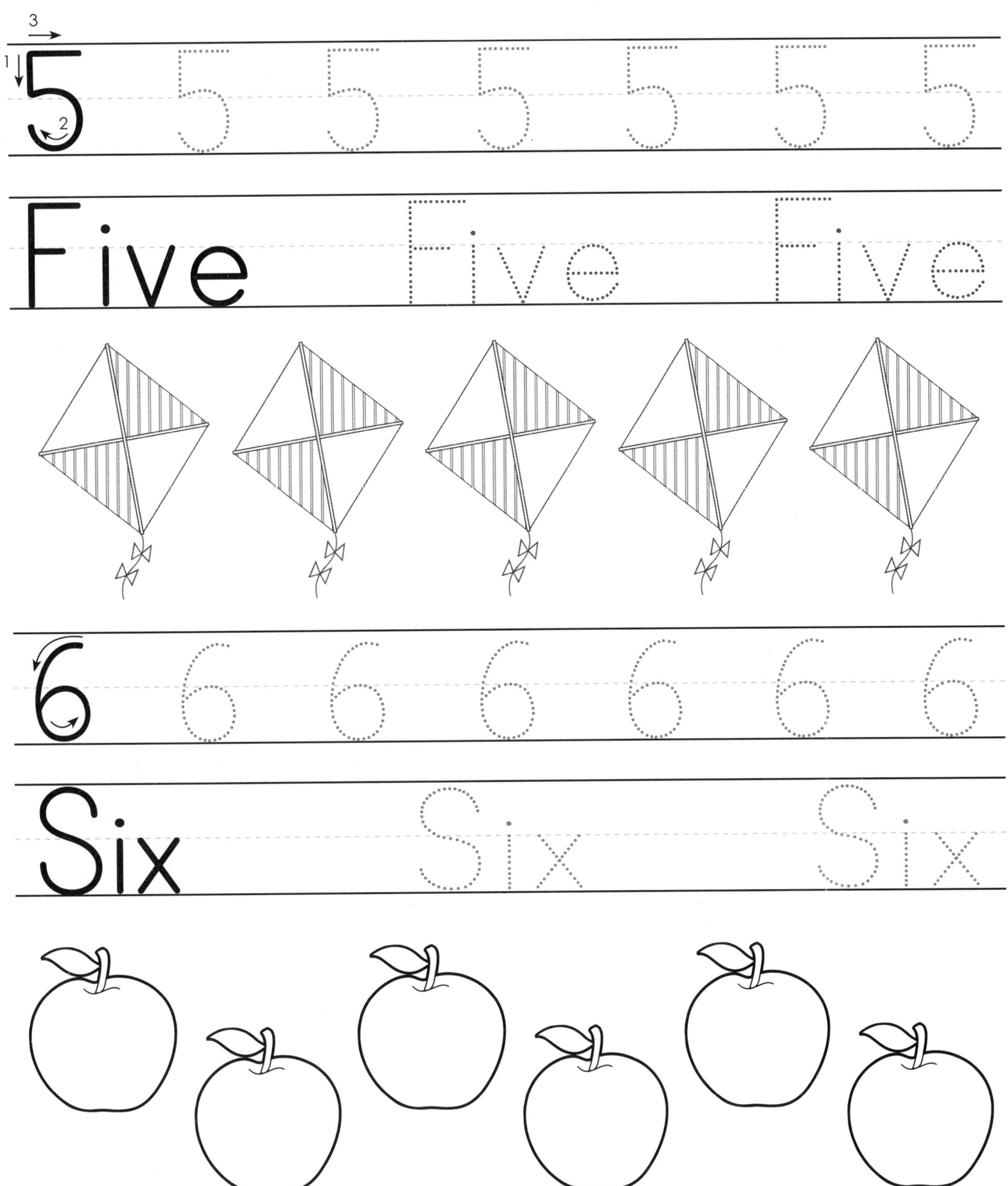

Trace the numbers, then decorate the pictures.

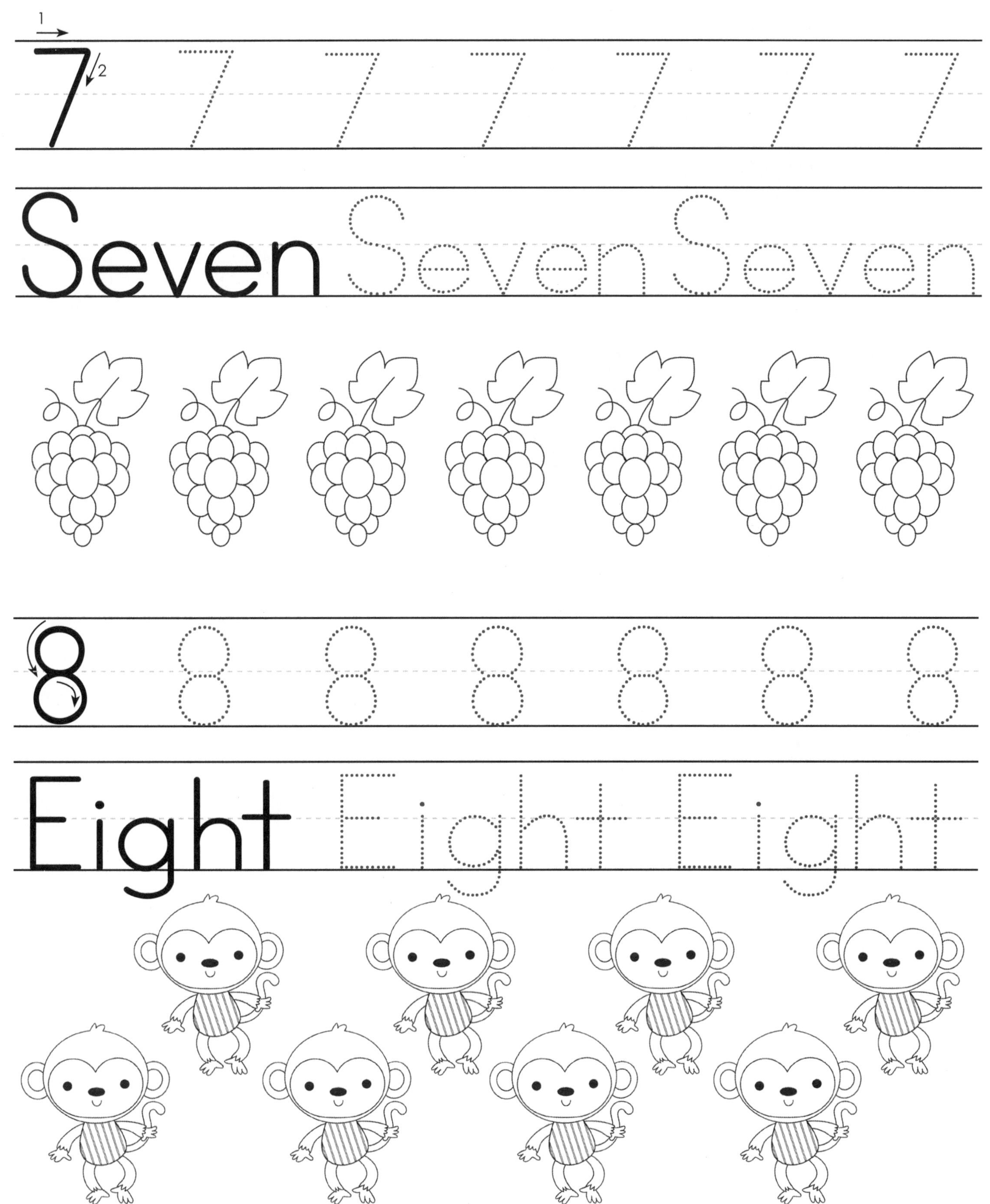

Trace the numbers, then decorate the pictures.

Write the numbers 1 to 10.

1 One 2 Two

3 Three 4 Four

5 Five 6 Six

7 Seven 8 Eight

9 Nine 10 Ten

Now practise your writing by tracing these words, then writing them again yourself.

tree

sheep

ball

ship

hen

train